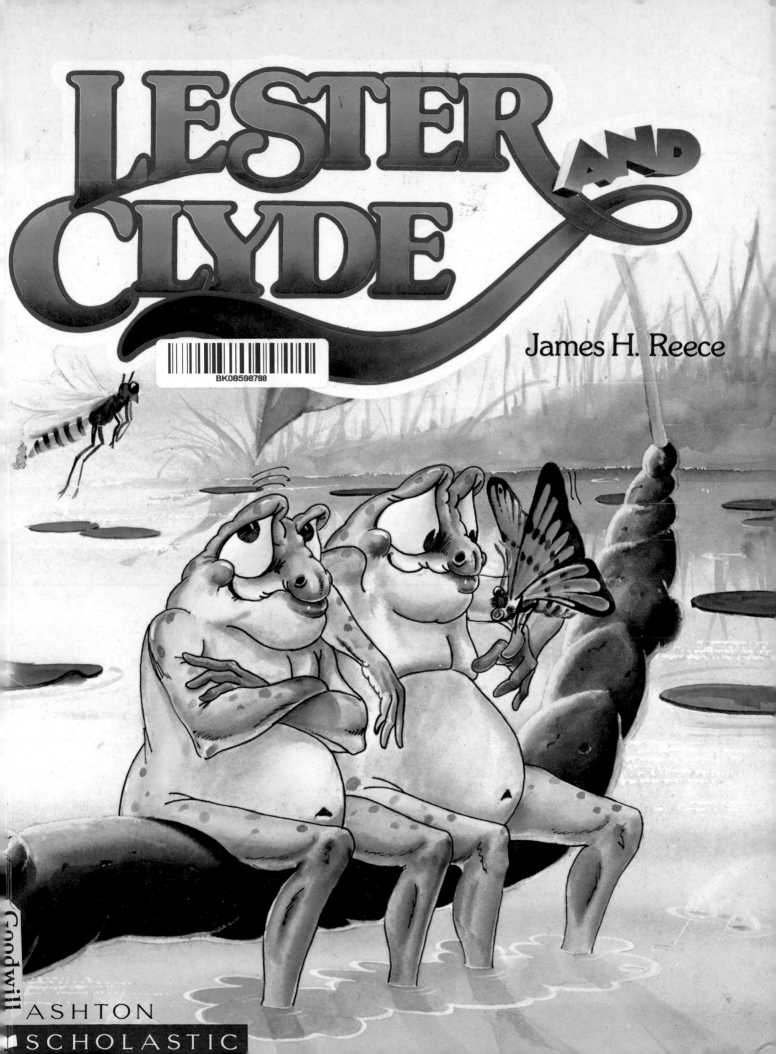

First published 1976
This edition 1991

Ashton Scholastic Limited
Private Bag 1, Penrose, Auckland 5, New Zealand.

Ashton Scholastic Pty Ltd
P.O. Box 579, Gosford, NSW 2250, Australia.

Scholastic Inc.
730 Broadway, New York, NY 10003, USA.

Scholastic Canada Ltd
123 Newkirk Road, Richmond Hill, Ontario L4C 3G5, Canada.

Scholastic Publications Ltd
Villiers House, Clarendon Ave., Leamington Spa, Warwickshire CV32 5PR, England.

National Library of New Zealand
Cataloguing-in-Publication data

REECE, James H. (James Herbert)
   Lester and Clyde/written and illustrated
by James H. Reece. — Auckland, N.Z. : Ashton
Scholastic, [1987]. — 1 v.
   Children's picture story book. — Reprint.
Originally published: Sydney, N.S.W. ; Auckland,
N.Z. : Ashton Scholastic, 1976.
   ISBN 1-86943-031-X
        A823.3
   I. Title.

---

16 15 14 13 12 11 10 9 8 7 6 5 4 3 2 1   1 2 3 4 5 6 7 8 9/9

Typeset in Century Old Style by Rennies Illustrations.
Printed in Hong Kong

LESTER AND CLYDE

Written and illustrated by James H. Reece.

Ashton Scholastic
Auckland   Sydney   New York   Toronto   London

Far away from the city
in green countryside,
live two fat, green frogs
known as Lester and Clyde.
Their home is a pond
that is sparkling and bright,
surrounded by flowers —
oh, a beautiful sight!

3

The pond where they live
is so peaceful and still,
butterflies flutter about
and birds trill.

The air is sweet-smelling
and perfectly clear.

It's a place where all creatures
can live without fear.

These frogs are no beauties —
they have spotty hides,
long, skinny duck feet
and white tummy sides.
Their mouths seem too wide
and their legs much too long —
they look like spare parts
put together all wrong.

Lester's the smaller
and he's full of fun —
a naughty, a nervy,
a mischievous one.
Clyde is much older
and likes simple things
such as beautiful flowers
and clear, bubbling springs.

One day when old Clyde
was asleep in the sun,
young Lester decided
on having some fun.

He croaked out his loudest
in Clyde's open ear
and Clyde leapt sky-high
in an anguish of fear.

CROAK!

This trick gave him such
an incredible fright,
that Clyde's bright green skin
turned a bluish-grey white.
But keeping his temper
in very tight rein,
he said very softly,
'Don't do that again.'

A few minutes passed
and Clyde stopped feeling mad.
He climbed up to relax
on a soft lily pad.
The day was so hot
and the bird notes so sweet,
that soon he was dreaming again,
fast asleep.

But fun-loving Lester
held up a sharp stick —
he was going to play
yet another trick!
He poked the stick up
through Clyde's soft lily pad,
which sank to the bottom —
and *then* — was Clyde MAD!

Spluttering and spitting
and seething with rage,
Clyde pointed and shouted,
'I've now reached the stage
when I cannot, I will not,
put up with you near.
You're a pest, you're a menace,
you cannot live here!'

They argued and bickered
and shouted all day,
till Lester said sadly,
'Oh, have it your way!'
He told himself smugly,
that in a short while,
he'd find his **own** pond
where he'd live in **his** style.

21

He set out in the dusk
and had not travelled far
when he made up a bed
in an old, broken jar.
Not a wink, not a blink,
did he sleep all that night,
for many strange sounds
kept him rigid with fright.

23

He dozed in the morning
and then set out late.
It was hot, it was dusty —
a thing that frogs hate.
Then he saw, just ahead,
a large, golden pool —
and wasting no time,
he jumped in, the poor fool!

He hit bottom, and then —
there are no words to tell —
his nostrils were filled
with a horrible smell.
What he'd thought was cool water
was browny, thick muck.
In panic he yelled,
'Someone help me, I'm stuck!'

But after a struggle,
he crawled up on the bank,
where he sat quite appalled —
his whole body stank.
In front of him lay
in the sludge and the slush
old, rotting rubbish
and mildewy mush.

29

Very sadly he thought,
as he trudged on his way,
of the pond where he'd lived
until just yesterday.
He pictured the flowers
of every hue
and remembered the water —
clear, crystal blue.

32

Later on in the day
Lester stood on the bank
of a pond filled with cans
and a squashed gasoline tank,
worn rubber tires
and an old, iron bed.
Such gross human habits!
They made him see red.

Disgusted and angry,
the small frog moved on
and found yet another
pollution-spoiled pond.

Its surface was covered
with greasy, black oil.
The decayed vegetation
made Lester recoil.

How he ached to return
to his own pond, and Clyde.
The sights he had seen
made him squeamish inside.
He yearned for clear water
and sweet-smelling air —
and the voice of a frog,
like himself, who would *care*.

Lester turned in his tracks
and he set off for home.
He'd been such a fool
and he'd felt so alone.
Oh! Never again
would he tease and trick Clyde.
He felt so ashamed of himself
that he cried.

On a branch by the pond
that was home, old Clyde sat.
He'd been mean to young Lester,
no doubt about that.
So he jumped with delight
when he heard Lester say,
'I'm sorry 'bout everything Clyde.
Can I stay?'

Lester gazed at the pond
and gulped down the fresh air.
He told Clyde that his journey
had been a nightmare.
He looked at the lilies,
the birds and the bees.
He knew then contentment —
how simple things please.

Then he asked Clyde, 'Why is it,
if **frogs** really care,
that men pollute ponds
and foul up the clean air?
They say **we're** no beauties,
the poor mixed up lot.
What do **they** know of beauty?
What **nerve** they have got!'

Clyde shook his head sadly
at all he had heard.
'What a crime,' he croaked loudly.
'It's simply **absurd!**
But try not to worry,
although it's so wrong,
at least we're safe here . . .

. . . until Man comes along!'